Anamata

AMY LAURENS

OTHER WORKS

ANAMATA

INKLET #47

AMY LAURENS

Inkprint PRESS

www.inkprintpress.com

Print ISBN: 978-1-925825-46-6
eBook ISBN: 9781393018216

www.inkprintpress.com

National Library of Australia Cataloguing-in-Publication Data
Laurens, Amy 1985 –
Anamata
58 p.
ISBN: 978-1-925825-46-6
Inkprint Press, Canberra, Australia
1. Young Adult Fiction—Fantasy—Dark Fantasy 2. Young Adult Fiction—Fantasy—Contemporary 3. Young Adult Fiction—Social Themes—Physical & Emotional Abuse 4. Young Adult Fiction—Short Stories

First Print Edition: December 2020
Cover image © Enrique Meseguer via Pixabay
Cover design © Inkprint Press
Interior art © Amy Laurens

ANAMATA

Adela huddled in the corner, praying nobody would remember she was there. The bedroom-turned-prison-cell was dark enough that she had trouble counting her fingers in front of her face, and the whole place stank of fear and misery, of human waste left to rot and fester, acrid urine burning her nose even as tears stung her eyes.

Her fingers were crammed into her mouth, something that usually would have been enough to make her puke with just the thought of what they might be covered in—but it was that, or let the sobs right out, and if she cried, someone would hear her, and if someone heard her, they'd take her out and torture her some more.

Probably they would anyway, and every tick and creak of the house cooling—it must be going night again; how many was that now? Three? Four? Something like that—might have been the sound of footsteps in the hall outside, coming to get her.

The first day hadn't been so bad. That was before they'd taken her and tried to break her—tried, because everyone always underestimated teenage girls, and they hadn't reckoned on her mental strength. She hadn't stayed alive for this long while war ravaged the countryside by being soft, or flighty.

And so: the first day had been bearable, even when she'd had to relieve herself in the corner, without even a bucket, because the room had been stripped of furniture except for the bare bones of the wooden slat bed-frame and a single sheet—which, in her darker moments, Adela guessed was there purely so that someone desperate enough had a way to end it all, saving their captors the trouble.

The second day had been tolerable, because for a brief interval, she'd had company: an elderly, wizened man so stooped he was shorter than she was—which, given she could maybe hit five three in a decent pair of heels, was saying a lot.

He hadn't talked much, and he'd smelled of sour sweat and vomit, and the bright red scars over his back and shoulders and arms—torture wounds, sliced open and immediately healed by magic, but healed wrong, so they never stopped burning—had brought bile in the back of Adela's throat. That was what waited for her, eventually, when they ran out of other, slightly less painful ways to make her talk. Ripping out her fingernails, for example.

But regardless, he'd been someone else to talk to—talk *at*, anyway—and something to care for other than her own pitiful situation.

Because the truth of the matter was, the only way she was getting out of this was dead, or else if they broken her mind so hard she'd never be of use to anyone, in which case they *might* decide to be done with her and throw her out into the woods beyond the enchanted fence—but then she'd be dead within the day anyway, of exposure or thirst or caught in the crossfire of yet another skirmish.

A few months ago, the worst thing she could possibly imagine was failing her exams, because that would mean admitting that she wasn't a real sorcerer, that everyone else was right and genetics mattered after all, and the fact that she and she alone could use magic but not detect other people's lies like all the other sorcerers meant that she was somehow lesser, inferior, unimportant.

The day she'd arrived at the famous Sibelius Sorcery Academy, she'd vowed that no one would ever have an excuse to call her inferior again, not after that prat Jiri Tahallin with his white-blond hair and ocean-dark eyes had stood up in front of the whole school after the welcome dinner and denounced her as a dud while the scent of candle smoke and pumpkin pie spice mix filled the air, and the taste of despair and homesickness filled her throat.

Screw him. He hadn't known her then—and he hadn't learned any better in the interim, either, even though she'd been top of every class, always spreading rumours about how she must be cheating, must be getting help, or—in the last twelve months, about halfway through sixth year when he'd turned dark and broody—that maybe she was sleeping her way to the top.

Although, to be fair, it was his awful crony Hydrant—red of hair, ruddy of skin, prone to gushing—who'd come up with that one, and the black-haired idiot Gully who'd done most of the spreading, probably to try to get into Tahallin's good graces.

But right now, it was easier to be angry than to try to make excuses for him; no, not just easy, but possibly a matter of life and death, as Adela sat cross-legged, alone in the dark, trying to breathe shallowly against the urine stench, leaning her forehead against the cold, splintery leg of the bedframe, picking at the skin around her finger-nails because physical pain was con-crete, measurable, tangible, and it sure beat the vague, amorphous anxiety thrumming through her head.

The door opened.

Adela's heart contracted, and for a fleeting moment she wondered if this was the end, if she was going to die of a heart-attack before anything else could even happen, never to know how the war ended, or whether everything they'd done had been worthwhile after all.

Then her breath caught in her throat, because the man at the door wasn't a man, he was lean and still a little gangly, his white-blond hair almost bright in the light shining from somewhere way down the passageway, away from where they'd stashed her.

Of course. This was his uncle's house, after all; it made sense that Tahallin would be around somewhere.

Adela let her head fall back against the bed post, pressing her nose right against it so the smell of the wood would mask the stench of the room a little more—opening the door had seemed to stir the air, so the smells that had settled rose and filled the room, even worse than before.

So Tahallin was here. He'd either come to take her to her captors again, or else he'd been sent her to do something himself, prove his worth to the side, etc. Adela ran her finger over the smooth, edgeless, gunmetal-silver bracelet they'd snapped onto her left wrist to prevent her from accessing her magic. Whatever he was here for, there was nothing she could do about it either way. He was plenty strong enough to overpower her physically, and she wasn't the only one rumours had circulated about in school—

That made her shudder, a tiny, contained movement, as she wondered if that was why he'd been sent here.

Tahallin was still standing there in the doorway, one hand gripping the doorknob tightly, the other flexing awkwardly at his side.

Adela looked up dully. "Whatever it is," she croaked—When had she last drank something? This morning? Maybe last night? She worked her tongue, swallowed, and tried again. "Whatever it is, just do it and get it over with." She let her head thump back against the bed post, probably ingraining a splinter in the skin of her forehead, and wound her fingers into a knot in her lap. "I won't tell you where he is, or what we've been doing, so just do whatever you've been sent to do and go away."

More than six years she'd spent at the school, fighting tooth and nail for respect, for dignity, for recognition. Oh, Bug and Leroy had been alright after first year, when they'd grown up enough to realise that having a girl as a friend wasn't going to give them cooties or make their balls rot off—

Leroy was even quite sweet, in his own way—but it hadn't dulled for one instant the knowledge that if Adela wasn't the best at everything she did, everything she'd worked for would vanish. No one would accept her into Society, and she'd live the rest of her life as an outcast, too magical for normal society, not magical enough for sorcerer Society.

Which meant she'd had six years to hone her mental strength and determination.

Six years of crying tears that tasted like salt on her lips, locked into the toilet stall that smelled of lemon cleaner and drains.

Six years of learning how to cry silently at night, into the clean linen scent of her pillow, while nine other girls slept around her, snoring and murmuring and muttering.

Six years of knowing exactly how to smile to send her detractors scrambling, because even if she hadn't quite perfected some of her hexes yet, they *thought* she had, and that was ultimately what counted.

Adela was a young woman who knew how to bluff—but more importantly, she was a young woman who knew the bounds of her own strength, so when she told Tahallin now that nothing they could do would induce her to tell them where Bug was and what he was up to, as he worked hard to solve the puzzle that would allow them to end the war once and for all, she was telling the absolute truth.

Tahallin closed the door, and for a second Adela wasn't sure if he was inside or out—she hadn't been paying attention, a bad sign, a sign that this persistent headache drilling at her eyeballs was taking up more mental attention than she could afford.

Weakly, she swallowed again, wishing she'd researched how long it took to die of dehydration, and what the symptoms were, in one of her late-night library sprees.

Feet shifted on the carpeted floor.

Inside. Tahallin was inside.

So. That was the play then. The rumours about him at school were either true, or else the adults had heard them too and had sent him here to make *sure* they were true.

Maybe if she didn't struggle, he wouldn't hurt her too much.

Was that a betrayal, though, of herself, of her integrity, to just lie back and let him... *do that*, without even putting up a fight?

Tahallin sat down on the bed, so close she could sense his leg next to her in the dark, and she felt the bed shift under his weight. "I'm not..." He cleared his throat awkwardly and snorted softly. "Hell, it stinks in here."

Adela opened her mouth, fully pre-pared despite the circumstances to give him an appropriately cutting re-mark—but he continued.

"I'm not here to do anything," he said, voice low and—was that a trace of urgency in his tone?

Adela tensed, waiting for the punchline.

"Well," he said. "I am, but no one sent me."

Even better. No one had sent him, so he thought he'd just sneak in and have his way with the prisoner while no one was looking.

Fan-friggin-tastic.

If she lived through this, Adela was going to make sure a bullet hit his heart the very next time she saw him, magical *or* mundane, she didn't care.

Tahallin touched her shoulder, a light brush—and she shrank away from it despite herself.

He hissed through his teeth. "Cut that out," he said, sharply like she'd done to him so many times in class.

She had no idea whether it was deliberate or not, but it grounded her like nothing else. "I'm not here to hurt you," he continued. "I'm here…" He exhaled again, and she sensed him shift. Probably, he was rubbing the back of his head, because that was a thing he did when he was frustrated.

Not that she knew that, of course. Not that she'd been watching him long enough to know. "Will you just… get up here, please?" He said it plainly, like they weren't in a darkened room that stank like excrement, where she'd been confined after being tortured by his literal relatives—like 'up here' wasn't a splintery, grimy, slatted bed and he wasn't responsible for six years of abuse and cold-shouldering by everyone at school.

"No," she said, because what else was there to say?

Tahallin hissed again. "Would it help if I said please?"

Adela ignored him.

If he'd come to hurt her, he would have started in the moment he'd closed the door, she realised. Tahallin was always absolutely decisive, acting immediately on anything he'd concluded as his right course of action—and she'd never seen him lose his temper, either, or fly into a rage.

So no. If he hadn't hurt her yet, he probably wasn't going to.

It was that, and only that, that made her straighten her spine and start unwinding her legs from where they'd been tucked up underneath her—right as he apparently gave up, slid off the bed, and joined her on the floor, back to the bed, legs crossed so that his left thigh ran parallel to hers, his knee against her hip.

He was warm.

She hadn't realised how cold the room had gotten until she'd felt his leg against hers, and a shiver ran through her—along with a whole pincushion full of pins and needles as the blood worked its way back into circulation in her feet and legs. She inhaled sharply against the almost-pain—and choked. Tahallin was right. It stank.

"Hey, hey." Tahallin's hand was on her shoulder, her back, while his other hand sought out her face in the dark, almost putting her eye out in the process. "Your lips are like paper," he whispered.

Adela didn't answer, instead rolling her lips inward—not wetting them, because she knew that would only make it worse, but pressing them together so she could at least pretend she was doing something.

They hurt, too, cracking and starting to taste metallicky.

"Here." Tahallin rummaged around in his clothing for a moment—Adela listened to the rustling, wondering if maybe this was it, if she'd hit the point of dehydration and maybe hypothermia where hallucinations set in, because this wasn't Tahallin, it couldn't be, he hated her and she was a prisoner of his family, and that noise sounded an awful lot like a bottle being uncapped and—her heart thudded—that was liquid, being poured once, twice, into something that Tahallin had set on the floor in front of him.

Adela twisted around, moving slowly so as not to bump the liquid—he meant to let her drink, surely he did, he wouldn't be that cruel—and froze.

Two tiny shot glasses sat on the worn, stained carpet, three-quarters full of a liquid that glowed aquamarine in the dark, bright enough to illuminate the space for about two feet around them, bright enough that she could made out Tahallin's features, see his white-blond hair, and the awkward, uncertain way he hunched, glancing sideways at her, eyes and mouth tight with… fear?

But that didn't make sense. This was his uncle's house. And Tahallin—Jiri—was never afraid. And his side was currently winning the war, and would win it for good if Bug didn't solve that puzzle in time to disable the weapon Jiri's side had, and…

And she was deliberately ignoring the point, because the liquid in the shot glasses in front of them… She drew her knees up to her chest, overly-conscious of how Jiri's left arm now pressed against her right one, a little sick that she was so desperate for human contact that his arm felt like comfort in the midst of a nightmare.

"It is… Is it really Anamata?" she breathed croakily, tipping her head at the twin potions.

He nodded.

"Whoa."

He nodded again.

Adela shot him a sharp glance. "Is it yours?"

"It wouldn't work if it wasn't," he said softly.

Which set her reeling, because he was right, Anamata did only work for the person who'd brewed it, but it had to be brewed fresh, and it cost nearly half a million dollars for two doses the size of the ones sitting in front of her, and holy *crap* did his family have money if that was the case.

"Why?" she whispered, fighting the urge to lick her sore lips, to tug on her filthy hair, to clutch his arm and start sobbing, because someone was sitting next to her, someone who wasn't trying to kill or torture her, and the Anamata in front of her was just a step too much.

"I need to know," he whispered back. "I need to know if I'm on the right side of this war."

Adela snorted. "Any idiot—"

"I know," he whispered urgently, shifting, but not away from her. "I *know*." He glanced at her, eyes almost black in the faint light from the potion. "Why do you think I'm here? But…" He licked his lips, and Adela fought to keep herself from mimicking. "They're my family."

Anger hardened into a knot in Adela's chest. "They're *murderers*. And I am next on their list." If only she had her magic right now. She glared at him, tugging at the band around her wrist.

He turned his head, meeting her gaze, and the sadness in his eyes nearly drowned her. "You think your side isn't killing people as well? Torturing them for information?" He shook his head sharply, cutting off her protest. "It's war, Adela. No one's ever right during war."

"Bullcrap," she whispered back. "The ones who are right are the ones fighting so it doesn't have to happen ever again."

Jiri smiled sadly. "That's exactly what my parents want, Adela. To never have to fight this fight again."

Adela clenched her jaw, swallowing back her words, because it hurt to speak anyway, and she didn't want to admit that he might be right. About a little of it, anyway, not about the war. "Why here?" she said instead, inclining her head at the potions. "Why me?"

Anamata was outrageously expensive to make, but if you could afford it, it was worth it, because one tiny shot like the ones in front of them would give you clarity of mind and foresight, a whole host of accurate premonitions, and for several months to a couple of years afterward, the unerring ability to know what the best thing to do was in order to reach your goals.

But there were rumours, too, rumours that if you drank it at the right time, in the right place, with the right person, you'd see your futures *together*, all the ways that you'd be involved with each other from now on, whatever they might be.

"Because," he said, gaze lingering over her face—and she inhaled sharply, almost able to ignore the acrid stench of the room while he focused on her like that, like she was the only thing that existed in the whole wide world, like he might hold her and never let her go again until the war was over, and the world was safe—"I want to know if I should save you."

Tears welled in Adela's eyes.

This was it, then. Her whole life, reduced to an uncertain fortune-telling by the most expensive potion on the planet.

And that was even *if* this was the right time, with the right place, and the right person—and the rumours about Anamata were true.

She nodded, carefully so the tears didn't spill over, just in case he could see them in the light. "Together, then?" She reached for the glass—and her grip on it tightened with surprise. She'd expected it to be chilled, but it was pleasantly warm, like a mug of hot chocolate on a cold winter's night.

"Together," Tahallin said, and lifted his glass. "On three."

"One," Adela said.

"Two."

"Three," they said together, and downed the liquid.

It felt like cold fire going down, and then like hot acid coming back up again as she coughed and choked on the spicy, sweet liquid.

She coughed, lips pressed tightly closed, once, twice—and then she couldn't help it. She coughed again, and Anamata sprayed out in front of her—but Jiri was doing the same next to her, and he was groping wildly for her hand, and she took his, and they gripped each other tightly as the room around them spun and whirled and roared, a riot of gold and silver and magenta streaks like they were in the eye of a hurricane, complete with the noise of the wind.

Above them, images formed and dissolved, like clouds in a time lapse video—the two of them together, in the prison room, Adela's hair tangled and matted, her skin sallow and pale, Jiri's eyes tight as he wrapped his arm around her.

The two of them sneaking out to the woods, hands clenched tightly together; the sound of rapid gunfire, the yellow flash of magical bullets ripping through the woods as they crouched and ran for their lives, pelting through the trees until they were separated, lost, alone.

A series of images that whirled past too fast to comprehend, resolving gradually into two sets of images, a his-and-hers as they wound forward in time, living their separate lives.

And then, an explosion of light, heat tingling over Adela's body as the images came together again, and Adela watched, horrified as they made love together in the whirlwind of light and the roar of the magical wind, and they *enjoyed it*…

Adela flung Jiri's hand away from her, crossed her legs tightly with her legs stretched out in front of her so she could ignore the heat pooling between them, wrapping her arms around her body and hunching over, dry-sobbing.

No.

No, it couldn't be the future. It was some sick, twisted vision that Jiri had made up to torment her.

He hated her. He'd always hated her.

And she... liked someone else, she decided in that moment as she thought of Leroy's dark brown eyes and wide smile and quick and easy laugh.

No.

Jiri was never going to be her future.

"Adela?" His voice was small and, in the sudden quiet, hesitant, like the butterfly touch of his fingers on her spine.

She bolted upright and glared at him. "Jiri Tahallin, that is not the future. It is not the future now, and it will *never* be the future."

He swallowed hard, and stood. "Okay," he said, holding out a hand to her. "Okay. If that's what you want... Okay. But..." He bit his lip in a way that was curiously hesitant, disarmingly adorable, and Adela despised him for it. "Can I at least get you out of here?" he said.

Adela stared at his hand for a moment by the light of the golden magic still fading around them.

But what other choice did she have?

She didn't have to believe it was the future. For now, it was enough that he did.

"Fine." Adela grabbed his hand and let him haul her to her feet, working hard to hide the wobbles as her head spun. "And then we go our separate ways, and I never want to see you again."

"Okay," he said gently again. "If that's what you want, then I promise. I'll get you out, and we'll go our separate ways, and I promise to never try to see you again."

Adela nodded, and let him lead her out into the light that burned her eyes, let him cloak her in his magic until they exited the house, slipped through the enchanted fence, and reached the woods, where, just as the potion had said, shots whizzed at them through the dark of night, and they ran, pelting through the woods with their hands clenched together until they stumbled, parted, and went their separate ways.

Only later Adela remembered the one piece of magic that she lacked, the one that every other sorcerer had: the ability to detect a lie.

Sorcerers never told the truth. And she was the only one who couldn't detect a lie.

THE MAKING OF
ANAMATA

In November of 2018, Liana Brooks wrote this fantastic story about two people who'd been enemies at school re-uniting as adults and falling in love. There's more to it than that, but the point is I really liked the story and wanted to play with that kind of idea too.

Also… Confession? This story is totally fanfic. Which, the idea of writing fanfic terrifies me, because you have to be consistent with characters you didn't invent and there are rules you didn't make up and OH MY GOSH SO STRESSFUL.

But there's a particular ship I appreciate for slightly complicated reasons (shouldn't be too hard to figure out who the ship is if you know the original text, I wasn't exactly subtle here ;)) and it fit with the vibe of Liana's story.

Inklet #26, *The Powers That Be*, wins the prize so far for being the short story that took me the longest to write; this one, *Anamata*, wins the prize for being the quickest. My son was at gymnastics, I was in the car for a few hours waiting, and this whole story just flowed out of my fingertips.

Although, another confession here, I wrote part of the story where they meet up as adults first. Then I backtracked, and within a week I'd written three sequential stories of them back during the war—the first three stories in what is now apparently a short story series.

Adela is one of my favourite ever characters to write. Her voice is just so intuitive for me, and I can't wait to write more stories for her.

A final note. The title, *Anamata*, is Maori for the time to come, or the future. I'd like to specifically thank Tata Stickland for helping with the translation.

There's a reason why the Anamata potion costs so much to make in this story world, and why it's called by its Maori name…

But that's another story for another time.

DOWNLOAD YOUR FREE EBOOK

When you buy a print book from Inkprint Press, we like to say THANK YOU by offering you the ebook for free!

Please head to www.inkprintpress.com/inklets/47/ and the use the coupon INK47LET to get your copy of this Inklet in epub AND mobi today!
(Coupon will only work once.)

Read more by Amy Laurens!

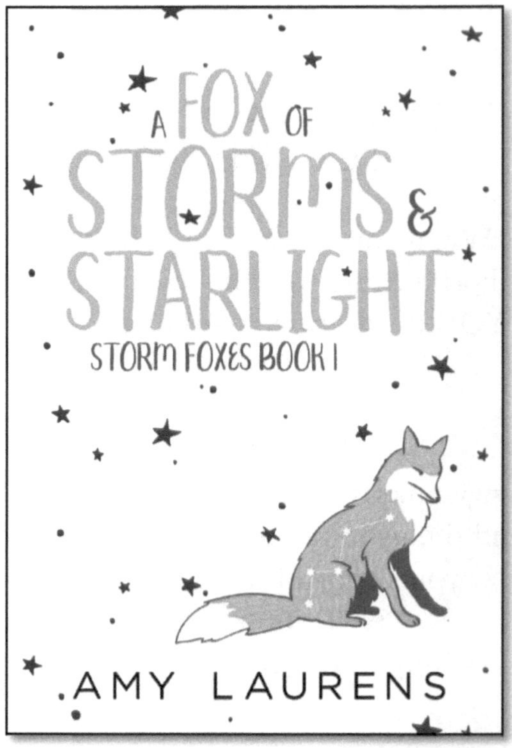

A FOX OF STORMS AND STARLIGHT

CHAPTER ONE

SIX YEARS AGO, I SAVED A FOX IN THE bush. It was only because my dog died. At the time, it felt like a pretty crappy bargain.

It was the first day of autumn—not by the calendar, but by the fresh bite in the morning air, the golden quality of the light as it lit the main road through town in the mid afternoon.

Sailor was a big, black shaggy thing, something like a Newfoundland, a lively shadow in the golden light, and I was eleven.

I'm sorry to be starting any story this way, but the fact of the matter is, this where it all began.

I'll spare you the awful details. Enough to say that Sailor had got out of the yard somehow, and had been hit by a truck careening down the highway that split our tiny town in two as it blatantly ignored the speed limit.

I saw it happen.

And although I cradled him in my lap as the smell of burnt-out brakes and hot asphalt and turning leaves filled my nose, his giant, furry black head all of him I could fit, there was nothing I could do.

There was nothing anyone could do.

I knew that, but it didn't stop the knot of frustration and guilt in my chest, or the taste of bile in the back of my throat every time I closed my eyes and saw the truck hitting him, again and again and again.

It took years for that vision to fade.

But that evening, only a few hours after it had happened, everything still felt fresh, and raw.

Sunny, my sister, was only nine at the time. She cried for hours, just sobbing like she'd never breathe right again.

I'd cried a little, at the scene with Sailor's head lying in my lap as his big, brown eye stared up at nothing.

It had been mercifully fast, there was that.

And the driver had copped a massive fine—speeding, reckless driving, I think they even defected his truck—and came to visit us later, a big, pot-bellied man standing on our front verandah, shuffling his royal blue cap round and round and round in his hands as he apologised.

But that evening, with Sunny sobbing her heart out on the couch in the living room and Mum and Dad trying desperately to console her as dinner burned on the stove, I couldn't cry, even though the acrid scent of burning soy sauce, scorching brown sugar and smoking rice wine from the marinade prickled the back of my throat and the corners of my eyes.

I was the eldest, and I had to be responsible.

Possibly, if I'd been just a little more responsible, Sailor wouldn't have died.

So I slipped out the glass slider from the family room to the deck while Sunny cried, glancing up at the two storeys of our moody grey house behind me before jumping heavily down the three steps from the rail-less deck to the lawn, and set out for the gate in the back fence.

I couldn't cry, and I didn't want to add anything to an already chaotic and stressful situation inside—but I couldn't stay there, either.

In the gaps between the gum trees to the west, the sky tinged to red and gold at the horizon, the sun sinking slowly into oblivion. I'm pretty sure I didn't know the word oblivion back then, but I knew what it meant, how it felt—and I craved it, desperately.

Anything would be better than the gaping hole in my chest.

And so, because I didn't know where to find it or how to get there, I stalked through the bush, pushing myself until I breathed hard and my lungs ached and sweat ringed me, chasing the way that hard exercise elevated me over my constantly looping thoughts.

Directly above, dark, heavy clouds obscured the sky, and the air was thick, heavy, humid.

Beneath the smell of dry gum leaves and even drier dirt, I could catch a hint of ozone, and occasionally the wind turned cool for a breath as it gusted against my skin, promising a late evening storm.

I walked harder, faster, outrunning the video looping in my mind of the truck's impact.

When the first drops of rain spat at me from out of the sky, I barely noticed. My skin was filmed with sweat, slick and salty, and the peppering of rainwater barely added to it.

That was at first.

But within minutes, it became clear that those first pattering spits had been the early foreshadowing of a storm darker and more intense than any I remembered.

Thunder rolled across the sky, distant and grumbling at first, a lazy background chorus to the rhythmic melody of the rain as it splattered down on grey-green leaves and red-tinged twigs, turning the silvered bark of an old, dead gum to deep grey and making the spiky, tussocky grass seem oddly luminescent in the dying light.

I stood under a grey gum with stains down its trunk that the rain was turning orange, arms wrapped around myself, shivering hard—and for the briefest instant, thought about not going home.

Mum and Dad would pitch a fit.

And I had to be responsible.

I turned, dark t-shirt plastered to my skin, dark hair sticking to my face and clinging to my neck, and began trudging my way back. The storm closed over properly, clouds rolling over the horizon and cutting off the thin scythe of blood-coloured sky, making the bush dark and unwelcoming in the premature night.

Lightning flashed.

Thunder cracked hot on its heels.

I jumped—and stared hard at the gap between two ghost-barked trees, where for a second, I was sure I'd seen a pair of eyes.

Nothing moved.

Nothing except the drenching rain, anyway, weighing down the branches that tossed fitfully in the wind.

The smell of wet dirt and soaked bark rose around me, undercut by eucalypt and ozone.

If anything had the power to wash away the hurt inside me, this storm was it. I tipped my face to the sky, imagining the rain washing over me had the ability to wash me inside as well, and the raindrops splattered hard on my face.

More lightning. More thunder, cracking over top of the constant hiss of the falling rain.

And in the distance, something eerie, lifting the hairs on the back of my neck: a strange kind of high-pitched howl, a cry that rang with moonlight and distance, cutting straight through the noise of the storm.

Bolts of lightning streaked across the sky—one—two—three in the space of half a second, followed immediately by a growling crack of thunder so immense it vibrated in my chest. I ducked instinctively.

There, in the corner of my eye…

I froze, crouched with my arms over my head.

The strange cries came again—and they were closer.

I stared hard at the place, low to the ground, where I was sure I'd seen something small, maybe the size of a cat.

Flash. Growl.

Rain spitting down.

There. Right there. A small animal, pointy ears, light coloured chin and throat...

The strange, eerie cries came a third time, and my heart pounded fiercely. Whatever was making the noise, it was close. Really close.

The little creature across from me reacted too, flattening itself to the ground.

My jaw twitched.

My heart pounded.

My fingertips bit into my upper arms.

Stay? Go?

Run? Freeze?

The hairs on my neck prickled again and goosebumps broke out all over me.

Cold dread formed a knot in my stomach.

Something was coming.

Something worse than the storm.

I had to get home.

I made it halfway to standing—and a series of strange, awful noises made me freeze again. They were sharp, clacking, squealing sounds, like someone knocking two echoing stones against each other, interspersed with high-pitched yowling...

And the creature in the darkness screamed.

I threw my back against the gumtree behind me, pressing hard against it. My heart hammered.

I peered back and forth in the dark, eyes wide.

Rain drenched down, but my throat was dry.

My pulse pounded faster.

The little creature screamed again—and as lightning flashed, I saw it on its back, legs slashing wildly at the air as something attacked.

The awful, clicking-yowling noises grew louder.

I slapped my hands over my ears, gasping. Water ran down my face, getting into my mouth, my eyes.

It was hurting.

Whatever the small thing was, it was getting hurt, and I'd seen enough animals hurting today.

Something in my chest snapped.

I flung myself across the ground, leaping a couple of tussocks and a fallen branch before I crashed to my knees.

I crawled closer, desperate, gasping for air through the heavy curtains of rain.

I couldn't see it. Where?

Somewhere here, near the base of that tree…

The yowling screeched right next to my ear. I cowered against the ground, spiky grass pricking my face, wet-earth smell smothering me—but now, there was a strange mustiness too, a cousin to wet-dog smell.

At the next flash of lightning, I saw it.

The creature was a fox—and something barely visible was attacking it, only the gleam of eye or flicker of teeth visible in the gloom.

But the damage was real enough.

The little fox's side had been opened right up, and in the bright, stark flashes of heavenly electricity, the blood was dark, thinned by the constant rain.

No.

No more animals were going to die today.

Not when this time, I could do something about it.

I snatched at a branch on the ground that turned out to be more of a twig, and launched myself toward the creature.

I had no idea what was attacking it, but I screamed and waved my handful of twiggy leaves anyway, batting them in the air over the fox like I knew what I was doing.

The horrible clacking cries ceased.

With one long, low rumble, the rain began to ebb.

Still gasping for air, pulse galloping in my throat, I sat next to the fox and shifted it carefully into my lap, realising as I tasted salt that I was crying.

I huddled over, trying to shelter the poor creature from the slackening rain, running my fingers over its wiry cheek—over and over and over and over.

"Please," I sobbed, throat tight and aching, chest constricted. "Please. Please don't die. Please."

Another gust of cool air washed over the clearing, taking the last of the rain with it—and lifting the goosebumps on my arms again.

I shivered, drawing the fox close, like it was a stuffed animal I could hug for comfort—its or mine, I couldn't say.

"Please. Please don't die. Please."

Something shifted in my lap.

Around us, the world stilled, dazed from the storm, but also something more, something watching, something waiting, as the bush held its collective breath.

The only sound was the occasional drip of rainwater from the gum leaves onto a fallen log—no insects, no wind, no rustling of leaves. Just... stillness.

And the fox, who shivered in my lap.

The clouds tore open, revealing a ragged triangle of stars that glittered in the fox's eye as it blinked open and stared up at me.

My chest snagged.

My throat ached from crying, and a headache was forming in the back of my head. But the fox blinked up at me—alive.

I ran a finger down it again, from nose to cheek to ear to shoulder, all the way down its side to its thick, bushy tail—and the wound in its side began to close.

Laboriously, it hauled itself to its front legs.

I tried to stop it—"No, it's okay, you can stay here, I'll look after you"—but it lifted its top lip to show half-hearted teeth, and staggered away.

As it did, I thought perhaps its fur began to shrink. And suddenly, it looked larger in the night—as large as a dog, as large as Sailor…

But I blinked, and it was just a trick of the light, because the creature that darted away into the bushes like nothing was wrong at all was clearly a fox, the size of a large cat or maybe a small beagle, and nothing more.

And if something screamed in the night not long afterward, and the cry sounded horribly, horribly human?

Well. I was halfway back toward home again by then, and I pressed my fingertips to my lower eyelids and prayed my parents wouldn't murder me for getting home so late.

Keep reading! Head to www.amylaurens.com/ books/storm-foxes/ to buy your copy now!

ABOUT THE AUTHOR

AMY LAURENS is an Australian author of fantasy fiction for all ages. Although her stories can get pretty dark at times, there's (usually) a happy ending in store.

As well as short stories, Amy has also written the award-winning portal fantasy *Sanctuary* series about Edge, a 13-year-old girl forced to move to a small country town because of witness protection (the first book is *Where Shadows Rise*), the young adult *Storm Foxes* series about Mina, who just wants to graduate and get out of town, and the humorous fantasy *Kaditeos* series, following newly graduated Evil Overlord Mercury as she attempts to acquire a castle—as well as a whole host of non-fiction.

INKLETS

Collect them all! Released on the 1st and 15th of each month.

INKLET #031
Welcome to Dark Dale
LIANA BROOKS

INKLET #032
When War Came to Town
A Powers Story
AMY LAURENS

INKLET #033
Not Fantasy
AMY LAURENS

INKLET #034
Courting the Winter Prince
LIANA BROOKS

INKLET #035
At the Home of the Winter King
A Storm Powers Story
AMY LAURENS

INKLET #036
With This Ring
AMY LAURENS

INKLET #037
Venus & Seven Reasons I Said No
LIANA BROOKS

INKLET #038
Oath Keeper
AMY LAURENS

INKLET #039
Forget
A Powers Story
AMY LAURENS

INKLET #040
NOT QUITE
Cinderella
LIANA BROOKS

INKLET #041
ONE BAD MAN
AMY LAURENS

DOUBLE ISSUE
INKLET #042
The Claustrophobia
Of Loneliness &
Adam, Be A Star
AMY LAURENS

INKLET #043
The Artist
as a Young Girl
LIANA BROOKS

INKLET #044
CONFESSIONS
AMY LAURENS

INKLET #045
But For Snow
A Kaldrios Story
AMY LAURENS

INKLET #046
The Boy
Named NO
LIANA BROOKS

INKLET #047
Anamata
AMY LAURENS

INKLET #048
A Wolf FOR
Christmas
AMY LAURENS